SPORTSLINES

THE OLYMPICS

by
Jane Duden

CRESTWOOD HOUSE
New York

Maxwell Macmillan Canada
Toronto

Maxwell Macmillan International
New York Oxford Singapore Sydney

Library of Congress Cataloging-in-Publication Data
Duden, Jane.
The Olympics / by Jane Duden.—1st ed.
p. cm. — (Sportslines)
Summary: A collection of facts and trivia about the Olympic Games.
ISBN 0-89686-624-6
1. Olympics—History—Juvenile literature. [1. Olympics—History.] I. Title. II. Series.
GV721.5.D78 1991
796.48—dc20 91-7278
CIP
AC

Photo Credits
Cover: AP—Wide World Photos
The Bettmann Archive: 4, 6, 43
AP—Wide World Photos: 7, 8, 9, 10, 13,14, 16, 17, 18, 19, 20, 21, 22, 23, 24, 25, 26, 27, 28, 29, 30, 31, 32, 33, 34, 35, 36, 37, 38, 39, 40, 42, 44

CRESTWOOD HOUSE

Macmillan Publishing Company
866 Third Avenue
New York, NY 10022

Maxwell Macmillan Canada, Inc.
1200 Eglinton Avenue East
Suite 200
Don Mills, Ontario M3C 3N1

Macmillan Publishing Company is part of the Maxwell Communication Group of Companies.

Produced by Flying Fish Studio

Printed in the United States of America

First edition

10 9 8 7 6 5 4 3 2 1

Contents

An ancient Olympic stadium

Inside the Olympics

Every four years athletes from many nations come together for the world's greatest sports contest: the Olympic Games. Scoreboards at the opening ceremony of every Olympiad display the same words: "The most important thing in the Olympic Games is not to win but to take part...." The words express the hope that fair play and good sportsmanship will triumph.

The pages ahead are filled with Olympic feats, firsts and facts. You'll read about many amazing and weird events. You'll be there for the excitement and drama of the Olympic Games in the 20th century. Let the Games begin!

The Ancient Games

The Olympic Games began at Olympia, Greece, in 776 B.C. Professional athletes—men only—competed in games held every four years. Each four-year period between Games was an Olympiad. At that time many people counted the passing of time by Olympiads instead of by years. If we still did that today and you were born in 1980, you'd say you were born in the 689th Olympiad!

Baron Pierre de Coubertin

The Modern Olympics

The ancient Olympic Games were abolished by a Roman emperor in A.D. 394. They did not take place again until 1896. The founder of the modern Olympics was a Frenchman named Baron Pierre de Coubertin.

As in ancient times, the Games are still held every four years. An International Olympic Committee decides where the Games will be held. The modern Games are open to amateur athletes of all nations. They compete against each other for prized Olympic medals of gold, silver and bronze. James Connolly of the United States became the first Olympic champion in over 1,500 years when he won the triple jump in the first modern Games, held in Athens.

The number and kinds of sports have not always been the same. Some sports have come and gone. Others, such as the dashes, distance runs, and jumps of track and field, have always been part of the Games.

The Olympic Games are a lasting symbol of goodwill among nations. In ancient Greece, during wartime, a truce was always declared for the Games. But there have been no truces during the Games in modern times. In fact, the Olympics were not held during the world wars of 1914–1918 and 1939–1945.

Sometimes politics gets in the way of Olympic traditions. An example can be seen in the parade of athletes for the opening ceremonies of the 1988 Summer Games in Seoul, Korea. The Greek athletes, true to custom, were first, as in every modern Olympiad (in honor of the original Olympics). The host team from Korea was last. The other countries marched into the stadium in alphabetical order according to the host country's language. But exceptions were made. Iran was supposed to follow Iraq, its archenemy at the time. But Egypt, Italy and India came between them to provide a buffer. In the Korean alphabet, Israel should have followed Egypt. But because of the Arab-Israeli conflict, Israel marched into the stadium well behind Egypt, following Japan. All but one delegation entered the stadium led by girls selected by the organizers. The Iranians, faithful to their religious belief not to follow women, were led by a boy!

Flying Colors

The famous Olympic flag made its first appearance in 1920. It has been part of the Olympic scene ever since. The flag shows five colored rings: blue, yellow, black, green and red. Every national flag in the world has at least one of these colors. The five rings represent five continents: Europe, Asia, Australia, Africa and the Americas. The rings are linked together, symbolizing the sporting friendship of all the peoples of the earth. The hope is that the Olympic spirit will rise above all barriers of race, language, culture, religion and politics. No country ever receives official recognition as the "winner" of the Olympics.

Symbols of the Olympic spirit: the flame and the flag

Doves of Peace

In recent years, white doves, a symbol of peace, have been released as the Olympic flag is raised. The 2,400 white doves released at the 1988 Games in Seoul, Korea, received a few years of special training for their part in the opening ceremonies.

The opening of the 1988 Summer Olympics in Seoul, Korea

Enriqueta Basilo carries the Olympic torch.

The Olympic Torch

The most dramatic moment of the opening ceremony is the lighting of the Olympic Flame. It begins with the Olympic torch being lit in the valley of Olympia in Greece, where the ancient Games were held. Relays of thousands of runners carry the torch through many countries. Sometimes it is carried by plane across oceans or mountains. The final runner carries the torch into the stadium, circles the track, and lights the Olympic Flame. It burns brightly throughout the two weeks of the Games. The flame stands for the search for excellence and the struggle for victory. The custom of carrying the torch from Olympia to the site of each Olympiad began in 1936. The 1968 Olympics in Mexico City saw a woman light the Olympic Flame for the first time. She was Enriqueta Basilo, from Mexico.

Welcome, Women!

The first modern Olympic Games, held in 1896, were open only to men. But by 1900 women were admitted to the competition. Eleven women took part in the second modern Olympics, held in Paris. The first Olympic women's title went to Charlotte Cooper of Great Britain. She won the gold medal for tennis.

Members of the 1988 U.S. Olympic team on parade in Seoul

The Marathon

The marathon race is a tribute to the legendary feat of a Greek soldier of ancient times. He ran with the news of a victory from the battlefield at Marathon to Athens, a distance of about 25 miles (40 kilometers). In the 1908 Olympics in London, the marathon race became longer. It began at Windsor Castle so the British royal children could see the start from their nursery. It finished in the stadium directly in front of the royal box of Queen Alexandra. That distance was 26 miles, 385 yards (42.2 kilometers). It has been the official distance for all marathons ever since.

I Thought I Could, I Thought I Could . . .

The 1908 London marathon turned out to be the most exciting race in Olympic history! Italy's Dorando Pietri came reeling into the stadium, exhausted. He toppled and fell. He was down for the third time when the second runner, Johnny Hayes of the United States, entered the stadium. Hayes saw he had a chance to win. Suddenly Pietri rose, then fell again. It was more than one of the officials could bear. He grabbed Pietri by the arm and half dragged, half carried him across the finish. Hayes crossed a few seconds later. There was so much frenzy and confusion that at first Pietri was declared the winner. Of course he was disqualified because an official had helped him. The gold medal went to Hayes. Six days later Queen Alexandra presented Pietri with a special gold cup for his valiant run. The next year Pietri and Hayes delighted fans by racing against each other in special marathons in the United States.

Won the Battle, Lost the War

Greco-Roman wrestler Martin Klein of Russia won the longest wrestling match in Olympic history. It happened during the 1912 middleweight competition. Klein and Alfred Asikainen of Finland wrestled for 11 hours before Klein finally won. But by then Klein was too worn out to compete in the final! The gold was awarded to Sweden's Claes Johanson by default.

King Bows to History's Greatest Athlete

"Sir, you are the greatest athlete in the world." King Gustav V of Sweden spoke those words to Jim Thorpe toward the end of the 1912 Olympics in Stockholm, Sweden.

"Thanks, King," Jim replied shyly. American Indian Jim Thorpe had given the greatest individual performance in Olympic history. He had won both the pentathlon (five track and field events) and the decathlon (ten events). Although Jim had never before competed in a decathlon, his point total was not surpassed by another Olympian for 20 years! Back in the United States, Jim was given a hero's welcome and a ticker-tape parade down Broadway.

Six months after the 1912 Olympics, Jim's medals were taken away by Olympic officials. His name was taken out of the records. They had learned that Jim had played basketball for a small salary in 1909 and 1910. At the time, any athlete who played sports for money could not compete in the Olympics. It was a crushing blow.

Thirty years after his death, in 1983, the International Olympic Committee lifted the ban against Jim Thorpe. Duplicates of his 1912 gold medals were awarded to Jim Thorpe's children. Most experts still agree that no athlete who ever lived could boast such all-around excellence as the great Jim Thorpe.

Hard Luck for the Great Zamora

The Spanish team was a favorite in the soccer competition in the 1924 Games. The main reason for this was its awesome goaltender, Ricardo Zamora. Before the Games, "The Great Zamora" had declared that he could not allow the opposition to score any goals. And he didn't. But the Spanish team was knocked out in the first round anyway. A teammate accidentally shot the ball past Zamora into his own net in the last minute of the game!

The Flying Finn

Beside the path that leads to the Olympic stadium in Helsinki is a statue of Paavo Nurmi, Finland's Olympic hero of the twenties. Between 1920 and 1928 he won nine gold medals and three silver medals. At the Paris Games of 1924,

Paavo Nurmi

he tried something no one had ever dared before. He entered both the 1,500 meters and the 5,000 meters, even though both were held on the same afternoon. Nurmi won both races within a time span of only 90 minutes!

Nurmi was the first long-distance runner who planned his races scientifically. He held one arm across his chest as he ran, carrying a stopwatch. Nurmi raced against time, knowing he could win if he kept a certain speed. He held the watch in his hand, timing his progress to the last second. Then he tossed the watch away as he began his final lap. No other runner ever held as many records or was supreme for so many years. Experts place Paavo Nurmi second only to Jim Thorpe as the outstanding track and field performer in Olympic history. And everyone calls him the greatest distance runner of all time.

Paavo Nurmi lights the flame at the 1952 Summer Games.

Tennis Tidbits

Tennis had been an event at each Olympiad between 1896 and 1924. Some strange things happened on Olympic courts in those years. In 1912 the players on the Swedish mixed-doubles team lost their edge against their German opponents. It happened when Swede Sigrid Fick accidentally smashed her partner in the face with her racket while reaching for a return. The Swedes lost. In 1920, ballboys were so disgusted with the slow pace of a men's second-round match that they left for lunch. Officials had no choice but to suspend play. The match ended up taking more than six hours to play over a two-day period.

Tennis was dropped from the Olympic program after 1924. It was brought back as a demonstration sport in 1984 and reinstated as a competitive event in 1988. Professionals are welcome, but no one over 21 is eligible.

Curtains for Rugby

The last Olympic championship in rugby was played in 1924. The United States beat the French. The Paris crowd of over 30,000 was so upset with the French team's loss that things got nasty. It took a police escort to get the U.S. team safely off the field!

The Winter Games Begin

Hockey, bobsledding, tobogganing, figure skating, speed skating, and Alpine and Nordic skiing have delighted crowds and produced famous names in the Winter Olympic Games. The first Winter Olympiad took place in Chamonix, France, in

1924. Sixteen nations and 294 athletes competed. By the XVI Winter Olympiad in 1984, that number was up to 49 nations and 1,278 athletes in winter events.

Sonja Henie practices for the Winter Olympics.

Double Good

The first—and only—athlete to win gold medals at both the Summer and Winter Olympics was Eddie Eagan of the United States. Eddie won the light heavyweight boxing gold medal in 1920. He then won a gold medal in the 1932 Winter Games as part of the winning four-man bobsled team.

The Other Babe

Mildred Didrickson could swim, dive, bowl and play tennis, basketball and baseball. She earned her nickname, Babe, because of her baseball bashing as a teenager, playing against the boys. They said her style was like Babe Ruth's. In the 1932 Olympic Games, she proved she was a track and field star too. Much to her irritation, Babe was allowed to enter only three events. She set world and Olympic records in each of them. Babe won gold medals in the javelin throw and the 80-meter hurdles. She won a silver in the high jump. She finished second in that event when officials ruled that her effort had been illegal. Why? She'd dived headfirst over the bar, a practice that was later ruled legal.

Mildred "Babe" Didrickson

Did You Say "Stella"?

Stanislawa Walasiewicz, better known as Stella Walsh, was a female track-star of the 1930s. A Polish citizen, she grew up in the United States. In 1930 she became the first woman to run 100 yards in under 11 seconds. In the 1932 Olympics in Los Angeles, she won the gold medal in the 100 meters. In 1936 at Berlin, Walsh finished second. When she ended her racing career, Walsh had piled up 11 world records and two Olympic medals.

Stella Walsh crosses the finish line.

In 1980 Stella Walsh made headlines again. Leaving a store in Cleveland, she stumbled into a robbery attempt. Stella was accidentally shot and killed. Her autopsy shook up the medical examiner and the sports world. What deep, dark secret had prevented Stella Walsh from smiling even after she had won the gold in 1932? Stella Walsh was, in fact, a man!

The Norwegian Doll

That's what they called the tiny blond figure skater from Norway at the 1924 Winter Games. She was only 11 years old.

Sonja Henie

She didn't win that year, but she went on to become one of the world's leading women athletes. Sonja Henie won ten world championships in a row through 1936. She won Olympic gold medals in 1928, 1932 and 1936. And she gave the United States ice-skating fever. Children yearned for Sonja Henie dolls. They begged Santa Claus for ice skates. They tried to skate like Sonja, who cut 40-mile-per-hour figures on ice with the grace of a ballerina. Sonja Henie dazzled the world with her skating.

You Ought to Be in Pictures

Johnny Weissmuller of the United States won three gold medals in swimming at the Paris Olympics in 1924. He won another two at Amsterdam in 1928. The Olympic Games turned out to be a gold mine for Hollywood talent scouts. Johnny Weissmuller went on to become Tarzan of the Apes. Buster Crabbe, U.S. bronze medalist in swimming, became famous as Buck Rogers. And Sonja Henie became one of the highest-paid and most popular movie stars in Hollywood.

Marjorie Gestring

Babes in Olympic Land

Who was the youngest athlete ever to win an Olympic gold medal in an individual event? Marjorie Gestring of the United States. Marjorie was 13 years and 9 months old when she won the gold for springboard diving at the 1936 Olympics in Berlin.

Jesse Owens Spoils Hitler's Day

Can you imagine an athlete with so much talent that he set five world records and tied a sixth in a single *hour*? Jesse Owens of Ohio State University did exactly that on May 25, 1935. It was the greatest day in track and field history. One year later, at the 1936 Olympics in Berlin, Jesse turned in another stupendous performance. He won four gold medals: the 100 meters, the 200 meters, the long jump, and the 4 x 100-meter relay.

Jesse Owens

Adolf Hitler, the German dictator, had expected Germany to win every medal possible for the glory of the Nazi regime. He believed that white people were superior to blacks. Jesse Owens, who was black, proved Hitler wrong. Of his 12 competitive appearances, Jesse Owens equaled or topped the Olympic record *nine* times and the world record *four* times. Hitler was not pleased. He did not congratulate Owens or any of the other black champions from the United States. Germany won 33 gold medals to the United States's 24. But Jesse Owens had spoiled Hitler's day.

Jesse Returns

In 1951 the people of West Germany asked Jesse Owens to return for a victory run around their Olympic stadium. The stadium had been untouched by World War II bombs. Once more Jesse stood on the platform of champions. This time he was warmly cheered and congratulated by German officials.

Jesse Owens recalls the scene of his triumphs during his return to Germany in 1951.

Thanks, But No Thanks!

The Turkish government was thrilled to have 11 medal-winning wrestlers in the 1948 Games. They were so thrilled that they showered their wrestlers with gifts, including money. That was a mistake. The Olympic Games are open only to amateurs. Because they took the money, the wrestlers were banned from future Olympics.

The Marvelous Mama

Fanny Blankers-Koen of Holland knew she was the best at jumping. She had set world records in the high jump and the long jump. It was time to try something different. So Fanny entered the 100 meters, the 200 meters and the 80-meter hurdle in the 1948 Games. She was also set to run the anchor leg on the 4 x 100-meter relay. Fanny proved she was not only a jumper, but a speedster! She took home four gold medals. Fanny was the fourth athlete—and the only woman in Olympic history—to win four track and field gold medals in one Olympics. American newspaper writers dubbed her Marvelous Mama. The Dutch housewife and mother of two became known all over the world by that name. She was one of the finest women track stars ever.

Fanny Blankers-Koen

Dick Button

Take That!

When Dick Button was 12 years old, his first skating teacher told him he was too fat and awkward to be a figure skater. But Dick paid no attention. He practiced eight to ten hours each day. Some weeks he didn't even take a day off to rest. His practice paid off. Dick's skating style made him a joy to watch. He saved his best stuff for the Olympics. In 1948 he became the first skater to complete the double axel. After that brilliant performance, showmen offered Dick up to $100,000 to turn pro. But Dick said no. He wanted to complete his studies at Harvard and defend his Olympic title in 1952. In 1952 he unveiled the triple loop: three complete revolutions while in the air. Dick Button is the last skater, man or woman, to win two consecutive Olympic gold medals (1948 and 1952). Dick turned pro after 1952, toured with the Ice Capades, and eventually became a lawyer and TV commentator. He also wrote his autobiography. Many say he is still the best figure skater who ever lived.

Al Oerter

Four in a Row

No one in the history of the Olympics had ever won a gold medal in the same sport in four Olympics in a row. Then Al Oerter and his discus showed up. Competing for the United States, Al won the gold in 1956, 1960, 1964 and 1968. In 1983 Al was 47 and still going strong. While taping a television show, he threw the discus an awesome 240 feet. In an official competition, that throw would have set a world record!

Feat for Bare Feet

The XVII Olympic Games were held in Rome in 1960. An unknown runner from Ethiopia amazed everyone by winning the marathon that year. Abebe Bikila was the first African

Abebe Bikila, running in bare feet.

Olympic winner. He set a world's best time for the marathon—running the cobblestoned route barefoot! In 1964, running in the Tokyo Olympics, Bikila became the first to win two consecutive marathons. This time he wore shoes! Abebe entered again in 1968 but withdrew because of an injury after having run one-third of the distance.

Never Give Up

In 1960 Wilma Rudolph became the first American woman to win three gold medals in track and field at the Olympics. She won the 100-meter and 200-meter events. Then she was the key runner on the 4 x 100-meter relay team. Wilma was one of the fastest women ever to run in Olympics history. Winning three golds was more than an athletic victory for Wilma. It was a miracle.

As a child Wilma had nearly died from scarlet fever, pneumonia and polio. She was left crippled. Wilma and her family worked hard for many years to make her legs stronger. Finally Wilma no longer needed leg braces and special shoes. Running was her joy. Could she be the fastest? Her mother urged Wilma, "Never give up." Eight years later, she ran for gold and glory.

Wilma Rudolph wins the 200-meter dash.

The Louisville Lip

Cassius Clay loved attention. He talked big and made jokes. Born in Louisville, Kentucky, he has been called the Louisville Lip. In 1960 he won the light heavyweight gold medal in boxing in the Rome Olympics. People were amazed by the 18-year-old's fast footwork and good reflexes. "Float like a butterfly, sting like a bee" is the way he described his style. He turned professional immediately after the Games. As Muhammad Ali, this boxer went on to earn the greatest amount ever by an athlete in a career: $68 million.

Cassius Clay receives the gold.

The Fosbury Flop

Almost every high jumper in the world used to roll over the bar facedown. This was called the straddle method. Then an Oregon high school sophomore named Dick Fosbury created a wacky way of jumping over the bar: headfirst and backward. People laughed. But not for long. His style broke high-jump records and became known as the Fosbury Flop. Since 1968 almost every top jumper in the world has been a "flopper."

At the 1968 Olympics in Mexico City, Dick flopped his way to the gold medal. His jump of 7 feet 4-1/2 inches also set the American and the Olympic high-jump records. Dick retired in 1973. He was elected to the National Track and Field Hall of Fame in 1981.

Beamin' Beamon

The high altitude and thin air of Mexico City had many athletes concerned about how they would do in the 1968 Olympics. But the thin air didn't slow down American Bob Beamon. When Bob soared past the limits of the measuring device used in the long-jump pit, he stunned the sports world—and himself! Beamon shattered the long-jump world record by almost 22 inches! His distance of 29 feet 2-1/2 inches was a great leap forward. When he realized what he had accomplished, Beamon suffered a seizure and fell to the ground in shock. But as of this writing, his record still hasn't fallen.

Bob Beamon crashes into the sand.

Peggy Fleming

Gold for Grace

Figure skater Peggy Fleming proved her poise at the 1968 Winter Olympics in Grenoble, France. The 19-year-old American looked like a china doll. And she made skating look a lot easier than it is. Peggy had trained with a great skating coach in Colorado Springs, Colorado. Practicing in the thin mountain air built up Peggy's endurance. Peggy trained eight hours a day. She won the 1967 national and world titles and arrived at the 1968 Winter Olympics favored to win the gold medal.

Just as Peggy stepped onto the ice for her freestyle program, the rhinestones on her sleeve caught on her tights. She thought for a moment that her costume might fall apart. Peggy stumbled a few times. Then she recovered to perform stunning loops, spins and jumps. Peggy's grace as well as hard work won her the gold.

Basketball Blunder

Sometimes Olympic officials make blunders. One they'd like to forget happened during the men's basketball finals in the 1972 Games. With three seconds to go, the United States had its first lead of the game over the Soviet Union, 50–49, on two free throws. The Soviet team's inbounds pass was deflected and went out of bounds. It looked as though time had run out and the Americans had won. But the timekeeper claimed that one second still remained. The Soviets were given another chance. Again they failed to score. At that point another official ruled that play had been resumed improperly at one second. The Soviets should get yet another chance to inbound, this time with three seconds left. The rest is history. Ivan Yedeshko threw a full-court pass to Aleksander Belov. Belov sank the winning basket. It ended the Americans' 62-game winning streak that had begun with their very first Olympic match. The United States lost its first game ever in Olympic basketball competition.

A Soviet player rejoices in the victory that ended the U.S. 36-year winning streak in Olympic basketball.

Tragedy and Triumph in Munich

Sad to say, the Olympic Games are a way for some countries to draw attention to political causes. A tragedy took place in 1972 at the Munich Olympics. Arab terrorists attacked the Olympic village and killed 11 Israeli athletes.

One of the terrorists at the 1972 Munich Games

The 1972 Games also brought moments of triumph. Russia's Olga Korbut electrified the world with the most appealing display of gymnastic talent ever seen. She won two gold medals and became a superstar overnight. It was this spunky, 85-pound 17-year-old who thrust gymnastics onto the American and world scene.

Swimming to Victory

In 1972 American swimmer Mark Spitz turned in one of the most amazing performances in the history of the Olympic Games. He qualified for seven races and won them all, setting world-record times in all seven. Will anyone ever top that?

Mark Spitz

The massacre of Israelis by Arab terrorists occurred the morning after Spitz had won his final gold. Since Mark, a Jew, was suddenly famous, people worried for his safety. Mark flew back to the United States before the Games were over. His career Olympic total of nine gold medals, one silver and one bronze is a record for swimmers.

The Most Famous Haircut in Sports

In April 1975 an 18-year-old figure skater sat in a hair stylist's chair. The 1976 Winter Games, just months away, were her chance for glory. But on that day Dorothy Hamill was thinking about her hair. After ten years of competitive skating, she was still looking for the right hairstyle. A friend had told Dorothy to try a Japanese stylist, Suga, on East 70th Street in New York City. Suga studied Dorothy's short frame. Then he started cutting. He cut the hair short in back to make Dorothy's neck look longer. He clipped the right side slightly shorter

Dorothy Hamill

than the left to keep Dorothy's eyes clear during spins, which she always performed counterclockwise. Dorothy was thrilled with her new look. Her hair instantly became her trademark as she went on to win the gold medal in Innsbruck. Soon women around the country flocked to salons for their own "Dorothy Hamill haircut." After the Olympics, Clairol hired Hamill to promote a new shampoo called Short and Sassy. And for the next 15 years, no one but Suga cut Dorothy's hair.

Olympic Salute

What did Daniel Bautista Rocha do after he'd won the gold medal in the 20-kilometer walk at the Montreal Olympics in 1976? Fans saluted him, and Daniel saluted his country, Mexico. He proudly donned his sombrero.

First Perfect 10

In 1976 Romania's Nadia Comaneci took the torch from Olga Korbut. Fourteen-year-old Nadia was a crowd favorite. She became the first to score a 10—the maximum score and a perfect performance—in the history of Olympic gymnastics.

Nadia Comaneci

Letdown at Lake Placid

They were America's perfect pair as candidates for the gold in the 1980 Winter Olympics at Lake Placid, New York. Tai Babilonia and Randy Gardner would be skating to defend their title as World Figure Skating champions. This was also their last and best chance for an Olympic medal. Tai and Randy had dedicated their lives to the dream of this event. But their hopes were shattered when Randy suffered a groin injury during the warmup for their performance. Their coach spoke the words they dreaded: "It's too dangerous for you to skate." Tai and Randy made one of the most painful decisions of their lives. They withdrew from the competition. Friends, fans—millions watching on television—all shared their grief.

Tai Babilonia and Randy Gardner

Boycott Burns Dreams

Who would win the medals in the 1980 Moscow Olympics? For athletes on the U.S. Summer Olympics team, lifelong dreams went up in smoke. When Soviet troops invaded Afghanistan in 1979, much of the noncommunist world, led by the United States, tried to impose a boycott on the Games. Not all countries supported the boycott. Japan, West Germany and the United States were among those that did. Many athletes were suddenly denied the opportunity to compete in the Olympics.

Mary Decker after falling during the 3,000-meter finals

An Unlucky Athlete

One of the unluckiest of athletes must be Mary Decker of the United States. Mary missed the Montreal Games (1976) because of an injury. She missed Moscow (1980) because of the boycott. Her dream race—the Olympic 3,000-meter finals in Los Angeles (1984)—turned into a nightmare. Mary Decker, 26, tripped over Britain's Zola Budd, 18. Decker fell, hurt, and was out of the race. Budd finished seventh.

Mary Lou Retton

Hello, Mary Lou

Olympic champion Mary Lou Retton practiced her routines over and over. "You should be able to do your entire routine sound asleep in your pajamas," she once said. "Without one mistake." In 1984 Mary Lou became the first American woman ever to win an individual Olympic gold medal in gymnastics. Her explosive style made Mary Lou, age 16, the crowd favorite and won her the women's all-around title.

Blue Jeans and Gold Medals

Levi Strauss was the official outfitter for the 1984 Olympics. The company designed the uniforms for the U.S. team. They also created one-of-a-kind jeans for each gold-medal winner. The jeans had buttons and rivets covered with 22-karat gold.

Valerie Brisco-Hooks was an unknown when she went to the 1984 Summer Olympics. But she came home with three pairs of special Levis. Valerie won gold medals in the 200 and 400 meters and the 4 x 400 relay. She became the first American woman to win three golds in track and field since Wilma Rudolph in 1960.

Valerie Brisco-Hooks

The World's Fastest Woman

She showed off more than her colorful one-legged running suits and gaudy fingernails. At Seoul, American Florence Griffith-Joyner flashed three golds and a silver. During the 1988 Summer Olympics Flo-Jo, as she is often called, set a new world record in the 100-meter run. Most experts believe that this record will not be challenged for another ten years!

Florence Griffith-Joyner

Jackie Joyner-Kersee

Jackie

The heptathlon is a contest of strength, speed and endurance in seven different events. And since it began, nobody has been better in this grueling contest than Jackie Joyner-Kersee. The long jump is one of Jackie's favorite and best events. Her strong leap in the long jump helped Flo-Jo's sister-in-law win the 1988 Olympic gold in the heptathlon. She also won the gold in the individual long-jump competition. The 800 meters is the most tiring event of the heptathlon. Hampered by a leg injury and exhausted from the competition, Jackie somehow managed to run the race in 2 minutes, 8.51 seconds. That was good enough for a gold medal and a heptathlon world record.

Steroids Cost Gold Medal

Canadian sprinter Ben Johnson won a gold medal for the 100-meter dash at the Seoul Summer Olympics. But tests after his 9.79-second sprint showed that Johnson had used illegal steroids. Steroids are drugs that can improve athletic performance but eventually harm the athlete's health. The once-scrawny Johnson had bulked up like a wrestler. In 1987 he'd shattered the 100-meter world record with a stunning 9.83-second sprint at the Rome track and field championships. Drugs did not show up in Johnson's system after that key race. But he was not so lucky after his medal-winning sprint in Seoul. His medal was taken away.

Ben Johnson (*right*)

Boost for Bobsledding

The United States has not won an Olympic medal in bobsledding since 1956. Los Angeles Raider wide receiver Willie Gault wants to change that. Willie was an alternate on the 1988 Olympic bobsled team. When he didn't win a medal in Calgary, Canada, that year, Willie set his sights on the 1992 Olympics. He talked two speedy and powerful friends into trying out for the 1992 Olympic team. Minnesota Viking Herschel Walker and gold medal hurdler Edwin Moses agreed to help Willie give bobsledding a boost.

The most important part of bobsled racing is the start, when sledders must run while pushing the sled. They need to be fast and strong. Herschel and Edwin had never even touched a bobsled before July 1990, but they are fast and strong. Coaches at the Olympic team tryouts were impressed. There's a good chance all three men will make the 1992 Olympic team. They are not talking about winning *a* medal. They're talking about winning the *gold* medal.

Atlanta Hits Gold

In September 1990, Atlanta, Georgia, learned that it had been chosen to host the 1996 Summer Olympic Games. The city celebrated with balloons, cheers, tears and fireworks. The Games will bring 6,000 writers and 16,500 athletes, coaches and officials to Atlanta from July 20 to August 4, 1996. More than 625,000 sports fans will bring their dollars to spend in Atlanta. Since Atlanta is building a new 85,000-seat stadium and other sports facilities for the games, 84,000 new jobs have been created to get the city ready. Atlanta will become the third U.S. city to host the Summer Olympic Games. The others were St. Louis (1904) and Los Angeles (1932 and 1984).

If Atlanta won the vote, what city came in second? It was the sentimental favorite: Athens, Greece. Athens hosted the first modern Olympics in 1896. The XXVI Olympiad in 1996 will celebrate 100 years of modern Olympic Games!

Residents of Atlanta celebrate.

Olympic Timelines

776 B.C.: Male athletes from all over Greece compete in the first Olympics at Olympia, Greece.

A modern artist's view of an ancient story: Ladas the Spartan falls dead before the judges after winning the Great Olympic Foot Race.

A.D. 1896: Athens, Greece, is the site of the first Olympiad—the Olympic Games—of the modern era.

1900: Women athletes compete for the first time in the second Olympiad, held in Paris, France.

1908: The distance for the marathon is officially set at 26 miles, 385 yards (42.2 kilometers) at the 1908 Olympics in London, England.

1916: The VI Olympic Games, scheduled for Berlin, Germany, are canceled because of World War I.

1920: The Olympic flag, showing five colored rings, makes its first appearance at the VII Olympics in Antwerp, Belgium.

1924: The first Winter Games are held in Chamonix, France, with 16 countries taking part.

1932: Because of the worldwide Depression, only four nations appear for the Olympic hockey tournament at the III Winter Olympics in Lake Placid, New York.

1932: The weather is so poor during the Lake Placid Winter Olympics that the four-man bobsled race has to be delayed until after the official closing ceremony.

1936: American Olympic gold medal winner Jesse Owens is such a hero at the Berlin Olympics that fans even shove autograph books through his bedroom window in the Olympic Village as he tries to sleep.

Jesse Owens salutes from the winner's stand.

1940: The Olympic Games, scheduled for Tokyo, Japan, and Helsinki, Finland, are canceled because of World War II.

1944: The Olympic Games are canceled again because of World War II.

1948: Fanny Blankers-Koen of Holland wins the 200-meter dash by seven yards. It is the largest victory margin ever in the event.

1951: Russia applies to participate in the Olympic Games for the first time.

1952: At the 1952 Summer Olympics in Helsinki, Finland, the Soviet team wins 71 medals, second only to the United States, with 76 medals.

1960: Soviet skater Lydia Skoblikova wins six speed skating gold medals in 1960 and in 1964, more golds than any other athlete in the history of the Winter Olympics.

1964: Australia's Dawn Fraser becomes the only swimmer, male or female, to win the 100-meter freestyle—or any other swimming event—at three successive Olympics.

1964: Between 1956 and 1964, Soviet gymnast Larissa Latynina wins 18 medals, more than any athlete had ever won in Olympic history.

1968: At the opening of the XIX Olympic Games in Mexico City, a woman lights the Olympic Flame for the first time.

1972: The Japanese sport of judo becomes an official Olympic event.

1976: Nadia Comaneci from Romania becomes the first gymnast to score a perfect 10. She goes on to score six more 10s!

1980: The United States is among the countries that boycott the 1980 Moscow Olympics. The boycott is in protest of the 1979 Soviet invasion of Afghanistan.

1984: Joan Benoit of the United States wins the first Olympic marathon for women, held at the XXIII Games in Los Angeles, California.

1984: Synchronized swimming and rhythmic gymnastics are performed as Olympic events for the first time.

1984: Greg Louganis becomes the first male diver in 56 years to win both the springboard and platform diving events.

1988: Tennis, dropped from the Olympic program after 1924, is brought back as a competitive Olympic event.

Index